D1442185

THE LITTLE
BLIND GOAT

Stemmer
House
PUBLISHERS, INC.

OWINGS MILLS, MARYLAND

Jan Wahl

THE LITTLE BLIND GOAT

Pictures by ANTONIO FRASCONI

Inquiries should be directed to
Stemmer House Publishers, Inc.
2627 Caves Road
Owings Mills, Maryland 21117

Published simultaneously in Canada by Houghton Mifflin Ltd., Markham, Ontario

A Barbara Holdridge book
Printed and bound in the United States of America
First Edition

Library of Congress Cataloging in Publication Data

Wahl,Jan.
    The little blind goat.

    "A Barbara Holdridge book."
    Summary: A blind goat keenly develops his
senses of hearing, smell, and touch in order to
save his sister from a horrible fate and to free
himself from being a slave to his handicap.
    [1. Goats — Fiction.   2. Blind — Fiction.
3. Physically handicapped — Fiction]   I. Frasconi,
Antonio, ill.   II. Title.
PZ7.W1266Li   1981   [E]   81-9429
ISBN 0-916144-70-4   AACR2

For RUBY CARRILLO
my favorite
storyteller

LIZARDS TOLD MYSTERIOUS TALES, and Little Goat stayed listening to them in the warm cave where it was cozy and dark. Hour after hour he stood still and would not move.

"Casimiro!" called his goat sister Todomira. She had eyes big as bugs. "Just look at the world outside. It's beautiful!"

She was right. There came new sun shining like a fresh mango, and butterflies and hummingbirds twinkled in hazy, soft blue air.

Yet whenever Casimiro the little goat hobbled on each foot to the cave's edge, staring hard as he could through eyes half shut and squinting, he saw everything swimming in a fog. He didn't truly see. He was a little blind goat.

"Let me stay here with my lizard pals," begged Casimiro. "They scratch my back if it itches."

"You are missing a lot," cried Todomira.

One day his sister nudged him, step by step, out of the cave down to the valley below.

But then she glimpsed an orange butterfly and she chased it over a hill.

The little blind goat stumbled into a cactus. Then he tripped on a tree root. He lay flat on his back with four feet sticking up.

He said, "I think I'll just lie here like this for a bit."

Pretty soon Casimiro got a new visitor. It was Don Fermín the grasshopper, who was called El Chapulín. And Don Fermín started to play his violin.

"Does it make you want to dance?" asked the grasshopper, fiddling.

"Yes, yes! But I can't see."

"It isn't necessary to SEE to dance," said the grasshopper. "Only learn to listen." So Casimiro struggled to his legs and kicked them up and he was dancing.

Don Fermín said, "I am tired of playing. But listen. Hear that hoarse croak in the yucca plant? That is Raven.

"Hear that sweet, clear song—which ends in a trill? That is Wren, sitting in a tree."

Casimiro learned to listen and each song made him dance in a different way. Then the grasshopper hopped away without his knowing it. The little goat was feeling better. Carefully dancing, Casimiro kept on going until he heard a splash in the river.

It was Doña Chana, La Rana, the frog, who croaked: "Jump in. Quick! The water is so warm!"

"But I can't see," bleated our Casimiro.

"Then follow my voice," called out Doña Chana. She taught him how to swim moving one leg . . . next, kicking with the other. He floated and rolled.

With her help, the little goat began to splash along like a frog. Then—all at once—Doña Chana was bored and swam off. Again he was alone.

"How lonely to be ALONE!" he sighed, stepping slowly up the high dirt bank. Shivering, our Casimiro shook his wet fur.

As he dried out in the hot afternoon sun, he brushed
into thin sharp thorns from a bush. And he groaned in
sudden pain.

Along waddled old Don Crispín, El Puerco Espín,
the hedgehog.

"What is this?" barked Don Crispín.

"I didn't SEE them," said the little goat. His eyes were
wide with sharp pain.

"Well," murmured the old hedgehog, "let me help you."
And while he was doing it, he said:

"First, learn to FEEL. Feel what is on the ground.
Feel what is in the air. Feel what is *near*." And Don Crispín
loosened the thin, stinging thorns.

"Thank you," bleated the little goat with relief.

"SHH," whispered the old hedgehog. "Something is moving, sliding across the rocks behind us. Oh, it is Rattlesnake!"

Immediately Casimiro's fur felt very prickly. Don Crispín gave him a nudge and both scrambled away.

Yet still, the little goat's fur was standing on end. "Who is it approaching now?"

"Just Coyote, prowling around up the hill," declared the elderly hedgehog, who promptly shuffled off to safety.

"I am alone again," thought our Casimiro. "But," he added, "if I don't budge one inch I may be invisible." Luckily, Coyote then trotted right past after poor unlucky Rabbit.

In the ground below him, the little goat heard the busy digging of Gopher. And above him in the soft air he heard the sleepy "zmm zmm zmm" of Bumblebee.

And soon after that he smelled something quite strong. It made his eyes begin to smart.

It was not Coyote but Don Leo, El Zorrillo, the skunk. "Hello!" said Casimiro, quietly laughing to himself, wrinkling his nose. The best thing was to be friendly. Casimiro walked up close and sniffed hard.

"What a keen sense of smell!" admitted Don Leo. "If you'll follow me I'll show you something TASTY."

So the goat easily enough followed the trail of the smart skunk right to plump grapes that had fallen in a hollow in the ground.

Both Don Leo and Casimiro nibbled happily without speaking until purple juice dribbled down the little goat's whiskers.

"Very delicious!" he told Don Leo. "Is it possible for you to show me another smell? Just as good?"

Don Leo pushed him to rows of tender corn. Casimiro stood on his hind legs, chewing one fine ear after another until his belly filled up.

Casimiro didn't learn until much later that Don Leo also had drifted off on his own business. Very tired now, Casimiro sat right on a hill of tough red ants.

"Ouch! They make no noise and don't warn you!"

It grew chilly and a wind blew strongly.

"Todomira," he called.

Rain plopped down. At first he liked feeling the drops, but then they plonked harder and he had to find a big tree to protect him.

All at once the wild rain stopped. And Casimiro could step out, although the tree was safe, like the cave.

After the thunderstorm, an amazing bright rainbow sparkled across a pink sky. Yet the goat did not see it, nor did he see the full, round moon when the sun finally fell.

Casimiro lay rolling in a pool of cool, soothing mud. "Lost and alone!" exclaimed the mud and fur. In the thick blackness of night the little goat cried loudly for his sister:

"TODOMIRA! TODOMIRA!"

"What is this?" hooted Don Calote, also known as El Tecolote, the owl, who came flying over.

"I do not see," moaned the little goat.

"Few folk are able to see at night anyhow," Don Calote called down. "Let me become your eyes."

If he listened, Casimiro could hear Fox's far-off bark. The scratch-scratch of Armadillo's long claw. Noisy Kingbird calling, "Chebu! Chebu!" And Quail's queer, late song, "Pitchwheeler!" Casimiro shuddered.

And he said, "Yes! Oh *do* be my eyes!"

Wisely, Don Calote turned his owl head this way and that way in all directions. At last he announced, "You can see *old mice* fluttering up in high air." (We call them bats.) "When mice die," he explained, "this is how they return to Earth."

Inside his mind Casimiro could watch them. "Go on. Do you see anything else?"

"Over there you will see," said clever Don Calote, "little *Washing Bear* down by the river." (We call her Raccoon.) "She washes everything that she ever eats."

The little goat laughed, imagining this. Then he begged, "Can you see my sister, Todomira? Really it is most important. To me."

"Hush, wait a second," answered the owl. "Be quiet. Let me look around." And Don Calote flapped gray-and-brown wings and rose high in the air and flew over the whole landscape, searching. Alas!

He returned, having to say, "I cannot find her."

Over Casimiro's head hung maybe a million, possibly two million glittering stars. The night sky spread wide like the distant ocean itself without any end in view.

How Casimiro's ears pricked up suddenly! For he heard a clear but very faint wailing. Even Don Calote, who had good ears, did not hear it.

And the little goat started to run, feeling his way as best he might, though he stumbled on rocks and stones.

"Where do you go?" wondered Don Calote, flying above him anxiously. "You said I should be your eyes. I see nothing!"

"You are wrong," panted the little goat, going into a gallop. Four hooves struck across the night ground. "My NOSE and EARS must be my eyes."

Following the sound of wailing, our Casimiro raced past bunches of wildflowers shiny in broad moonlight. He tripped. Over and over again. But each time he picked himself up, breathless. He would stop and listen, sniffing the night air.

A doubting Don Calote followed above the blind goat. Upon a rocky hillside, her hind legs now tightly tethered to a short and skinny tree, Todomira stood calling her brother:

"Casimiro!"

"What happened?" he asked her when he was able to catch his breath. She replied:

"One of the Man-folk found me and dragged me here." She uttered another low wail. And she truly hardly believed it was Casimiro until he licked her face and ears.

"Soon HE will return for me—early at sun-up—I fear!" she sobbed.

Chewing steadily with sharp teeth, her little blind brother broke the green vines binding her.

Todomira rubbed close, growing calm.

"I ought to watch you better," she bleated. "I never caught the orange butterfly."

Only she heard him snicker, "I must watch after *you*."

That wise owl Don Calote, gray as the last streaks of the night sky, hooted nothing at all but flew off, watching out for Man-folk.

The two little goats rested. Then they raced back to the cave to tell stories to the silly stay-at-home lizards.

How to Say the Names

CASIMIRO	Kaz-ee-MEE-row
TODOMIRA	Tow-dow-MEE-ra
DON FERMIN,	Don Fare-MEEN
EL CHAPULIN (grasshopper)	el Chap-oo-LEEN
DONA CHANA,	Don-ya CHA-nah
LA RANA (frog)	la RAH-nah
DON CRISPIN,	Don Crees-PEEN
EL PUERCO ESPIN (hedgehog)	el PWER-ko Es-PEEN
DON LEO,	Don LAY-o
EL ZORRILLO (skunk)	el Zore-EE-yo
DON CALOTE,	Don Ka-LOW-tay
EL TECOLOTE (owl)	el Teck-o-LOW-tay

Designed by Antonio Frasconi
Composed in Bodoni Roman by the Service Composition Company,
Baltimore, Maryland
Color separations by Capper, Inc., Knoxville, Tennessee,
Printed on 80 lb. Mead Moistrite Matte by
Rugby, Inc., Knoxville, Tennessee
Bound in Kingston Natural Finish by Delmar Printing Company,
Charlotte, North Carolina